OOMSBURY BOOK

BELONGS TO

....

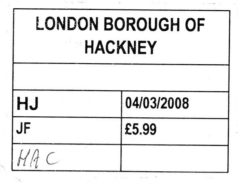

TO GRANDMA X

First published in Great Britain in 2007 by Bloomsbury Publishing Plc
36 Soho Square, London, W1D 3QY

Text and illustrations copyright © 2007 Natalie Russell
The moral right of the author has been asserted

A CIP catalogue record of this book is available from the British Library

ISBN 978 0 7475 8319 6

Printed in China

1 3 5 7 9 10 8 6 4 2

cover design by Nina Tara

www.bloomsbury.com

FSC Mixed Sources
Product group from well-managed
forests, and other controlled sources
www.fsc.org Cert no. SCS-COC-00927
© 1996 Forest Stewardship Council

Home sweet Hamish

NATALIE RUSSELL

BLOOMSBURY
CHILDREN'S
BOOKS

It was a cold and wintry day. The wind blew the falling snow through the glen, but Cat, Squirrel and Rabbit were snug and warm inside their cosy house.

Cat, Squirrel and Rabbit were very proud of their little house. It was their home and it was the perfect place to live. Until . . .

HAMISH
came to stay.

Cat, Squirrel and Rabbit
loved Hamish, but he
was big and hairy with
huge horns and more
bad habits than the
animals could bear.

Hamish was VERY CLUMSY . . .
He was always knocking things over.

HAMISH!

He was REALLY LAZY . . .
Always leaving things lying around (including
his toffee wrappers - very sticky!)

And he was TERRIBLY UNTIDY . . .
Always trailing things in and out,
in and out,
and in and out!

And when the animals said,
"Hamish, tidy up your mess!"
he huffed and puffed and
grumped and moaned.

TUT!

Then one day, Hamish caused absolute CHAOS. He knocked everything over, and the animals went crazy!

"**THAT'S IT!**" yelled Rabbit.
"We've had it up to here!" shouted Squirrel.
"We can't cope with your mess any more!" cried Cat.
And they packed Hamish's toffee bag and sent him out into the snow.

OUT!

Hamish couldn't understand what all the fuss was about.
"It was only a few wrappers," he whined.

And, feeling sorry for himself, Hamish sat down in the snow and ate some toffee. Because a toffee or two always made him feel much better.

After the animals had tidied away Hamish's mess,
they relaxed and put their feet up.
The house was so peaceful without Hamish.

As the day wore on,
the snowflakes grew
bigger. The animals started
to feel guilty.

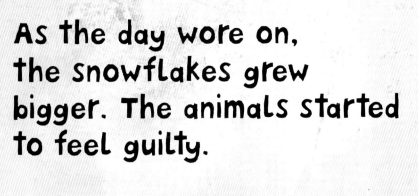

"Poor Hamish!" murmured Rabbit.
"We can't just leave him out
there!" said Cat.
"But he can't live HERE!"
insisted Squirrel.

Still, they all agreed that something
had to be done.
So they set to work on a plan.

Suddenly, the animals' front door flew open, and cat, Squirrel and Rabbit rushed outside into the snow.

"HAMISH . . .

WE HAVE AN IDEA!"
they cried.

And they raced after Hamish and showed him their plan.

PLAN

The plan was simple, but the animals needed someone big and strong to make it work.
"Hamish, will you help us?" they asked.
"I'll do my best!" beamed Hamish.
So the animals explained what they needed him to do.

Hamish gathered as much wood as he could carry.

And Cat, Squirrel and Rabbit searched for some handy bits and bobs on Hamish's piles of rubbish.

Then, while the animals held the pieces in place, Hamish hammered them together with his hard hooves.

BANG!
BANG!

And after lots of clattering and banging, and some special finishing touches, there stood . . .

JAM

There was plenty of room for all his things, a special tin for his toffees and even a little door leading into the animals' house next door.

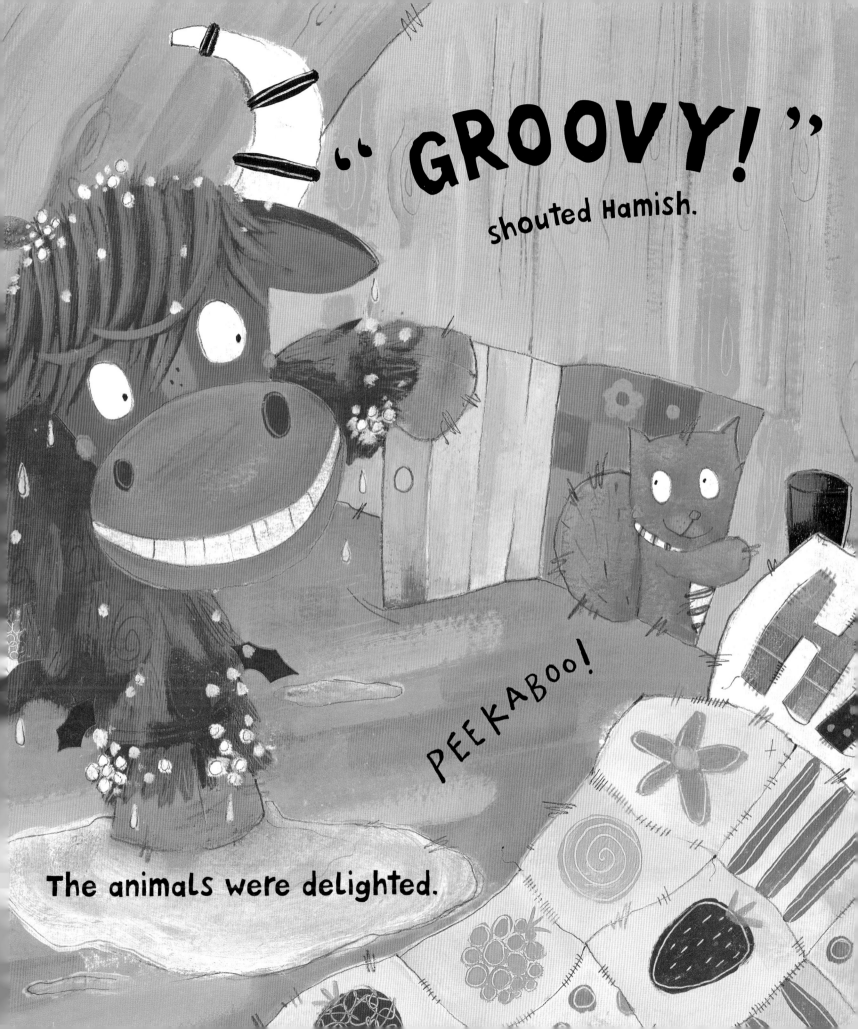

Hamish unpacked his bag and made himself at home.
"Would you like to come round for toffee?"
asked Hamish.
"Mmmm . . . yes, please!" said the animals.

"Do come in, then," beamed Hamish.
"But make sure you **wipe your feet!**"